ẸLẸ́MỌ̀ṢỌ́ MUST DIE

KOLADE FOLAMI

IMPERIAL PUBLISHERS LIMITED
IBADAN

Library of the Congress Control Number: 2023903818

ISBN 9789785207743

For Bolaji, Labanji and Jibola.

The tripod balances the pot of existence.

TABLE OF CONTENTS

CHARACTERS

1. **ELEMOSO**

   An Army General for the Alaafin of Oyo and the Commander of the King's Guard.

2. **ALAAFIN**

   The Paramount ruler of the old Oyo empire.

3. **AJIUN**

   The mother of Elemosho.

4. **GENERAL EGUNU**

   The female warlord of the Nupe Kingdom

5. **JEBATA**

   Alaafin's General

6. **AJANGBADI**

   Alaafin's General

7. SUNU

Alaafin's General and a native of Bariba in the Borgu kingdom.

8. ERUKU-INA

Alaafin's General

9. BALOGUN-PARAKOYI

Alaafin's Chief of commerce

10. ELENTE

The King of Nupe Kingdom

11. NDAEJI

A chief in the Nupe kingdom

12. UBANDAWAKI

The Male General of Nupe

13. ROYAL BARD

14. COMMANDER

15. SOLDIERS

16. YORUBA SUBALTERN

17. OYO SOLDIERS

18. FIVE HEFTY MEN

19. VILLAGE PEOPLE

20. TRADER ONE

21. TRADER TWO

22. TRADERS

23. FIVE HEFTY MEN

24. DIVINER

25. MALAOLU

26. MOLUYI

Malaolu's niece.

27. RUNNERS

28. WARDER

29. PRISONER

30. IDOWU

31. CHORUS

32. ALAKUTA

Member of Eso clan of warriors

33. ADAGUNODO

Member of the Eso clan of warriors

34. AKILAPA ESO IKOYI

The ancestor of Elemoso

The deft use of lights should accompany the embedded liminalities in the play. The drumming should be martial, and the volume should be reduced or increased as demanded by the pace of the actions.

ACT ONE

SCENE ONE

The scene depicts a room. There is Elemoso, clad in a loin cloth. Two men, Alakuta and Adagunodo enter the stage to confront Elemoso.

Both men also have their upper torso exposed but unlike Elemoso, they wear skirt-like trousers that reach the floor. Adagunodo addresses Elemoso.

ADAGUNODO: Elemoso, this is the final lap of the rites.

[*He hands over to him a black cap*].

This is the cap of the Eso. You have become one of us.

ALAKUTA: Indeed, you have become one of us. We are the guardians of Oyo.

ELEMOSO: I give thanks to you.

ADAGUNODO: The time has come to enter the closet and have supper with the panther. Are you ready?

ELEMOSO: I am ready. I have been waiting for nothing else all my life.

The stage becomes dark and when the light returns, it is focused on Elemoso. A large man, with the skin of a leopard as a dress, enters the stage and Elemoso falls on his knees.

ELEMOSO: Iba oooo[1]! Iba! My father Akilapa Eso Ikoyi, I am before you in reverence.

AKILAPA: Why have you come to seek me? The dead do not engage in palaver with the living.

ELEMOSO: Unassailable, the truth you have spoken, my father. I know you are not with us anymore, but you have never left us since you departed. That I may be like you, I have come to you.

---

[1] I adore you.

AKILAPA: [*Roars like a lion and slow drumming accompanies the roaring. The roaring stops abruptly*] Elemoso!

ELEMOSO: My father, I answer you.

AKILAPA: You must never betray Oyo.

ELEMOSO: I promise you this, my father: I shall never betray Oyo.

Curtain Closes

SCENE TWO

The curtain opens to a scene of fleeing and confused soldiers. Their feet are unshod, the majority are clad in broad skirt-like trousers and leathery breastplates that are clasped on the upper torso like a waistcoat. They carry machetes and broad-basket-like shields.

The curtain closes briefly and opens once more to a scene of another group of soldiers who are armed with swords, long lances, bows, and arrows in the quiver, apparently pursuing the fleeing soldiers. Martial drumming builds up in the background.

The stage becomes dark again briefly, and the light gradually brightens, and it focuses on Elemoso, a tall, bearded, and well-built man, standing resolutely in the middle of the stage.

The martial drumming, combined with the cacophonic noise of Yoruba and Nupe words gradually subsides as the light is fully on the man.

ELEMOSO: The fiercest of the battle is the test of the brave. I, Elemoso, stand and I become the hill unshakeable and unmovable. I have lived in the shadows of death but today I step into its full glare.

I have covenanted with pony-tailed apparitions that I may enter the house of the devourer with the shrill cry of fury.

I am Eso, the one who makes safe the innermost chambers of the *Alaafin*.

[*He becomes angry and increases the volume of his voice*].

Who is the protector if he cannot welcome the arrival of the volleys with bare-chested panache?

His part of the stage gradually becomes dark while the light gradually increases on the pursuing soldiers who were running but stop, on seeing something in their front. A commander steps forward.

COMMANDER: Ekpa![2] [*The soldiers remove arrows from their quivers and attach them to the taut bowstrings and they pull*]

COMMANDER: Cé![3]

[*The Soldiers shoot the arrows upward and the scene becomes dark. The light brightens on Elemoso, still standing but this time his body is riddled with arrows,*

---

[2] Arrows!

[3] Fire!

and he looks like a porcupine. The soldiers move towards him briskly, but they stop suddenly]

ELEMOSO: [*Laughs gutturally and talks in between gasps*] They asked for the company of the balladeers, but they got for their bargain the jostling of sixteen hundred mothers of scorpions.

[*He laughs again, and he moves to meet them*]

SOLDIERS: [*In unison*] **Alijenu**![4] Ghost! Alijenu! Alijenu! Alijenu! Alijenu!

[*And they start to flee, running away from the porcupine-like figure. The light focuses on the fleeing Yoruba soldiers as they are stopping when they heard the noise from the Nupe soldiers. Immediately one of the soldiers, apparently a subaltern starts shouting at the top of his lungs*]

YORUBA SUBALTERN: Elemoso ti duro! Elemoso has stood! Elemoso faced them! Oyo let us return!

[*He starts to run in the direction of the fleeing Nupe Soldiers on the stage*]

OYO SOLDIERS: Oyo let us return! Oyo let us go! Oyo let us go back!

---

[4] Ghost!

[*They speedily follow the subaltern, and the stage briefly darkens. The light brightens and the stage becomes a scene of a fierce sword fight between Oyo and Nupe soldiers. The stage darkens again as the light focuses on the far-left part of the stage. An equestrian figure gradually emerges. The female rider dismounts quickly and draws out her sword. She walks towards the grinning and arrow-riddled Elemoso*]

GENERAL EGUNU: So, it was you who had the effrontery to shift the grounds from the feet of my soldiers?

[*She peered into Elemoso's fixed gaze, and she hissed*]

This would not have happened if that clumsy Abugi had allowed the undefeatable Egunu to oversee the battle today, but he wants the glory.

[*She pauses to briefly survey the stage to see many soldiers lying dead or in the final throes of life. Elemoso coughs*]

ELEMOSO: You, you? [*He coughs again*]

GENERAL EGUNU: Oh! You are still living? I thought they said that you are an apparition.

[*She sheathes her sword and starts to remove the arrows that stuck into Elemoso's chest while Elemoso made painfilled grunts*]

There is no kindness in my act, for I shall take you to Nupeland where your sinews shall be mixed with **buruzàgi**[5] **for** the Elente's morning brews.

[*With an uncommon strength she lifts Elemoso and places him in a sitting position on the back of the horse. Then she steps on the stirrup and mounts the horse also. She clasps Elemoso's arms around her abdomen and binds it together with a rope. She cudgels the horse with her boot*]

Heyah! Heyah! Heyah!

[*And she rides swiftly away from the stage as the curtain closes*]

---

[5] Local spiced beer

SCENE THREE

Five hefty men run to meet the horse rider who had stopped in the middle of the stage and is dismounting. They help her with the wounded and a probably dead man that was clasped to her on the horse. In the background were children, women, and some old men who mind their business as they steal glances at the General and her receiving party.

FIVE HEFTY MEN: [*In unison*] **Bèrènyi!**[6] Welcome! **Bèrènyi!** Welcome!

Egunnu nods in acknowledgment of the greetings, and surveys the mass of humanity in the background, while the men lift the wounded Elemoso and place him on the shoulder of one of them and they exit the stage briskly.

EGUNNU: Wawa![7] **Edagi!**[8] Fools!

[*Egunnu thunders angrily. Instantly all the women, children, and old men rise and curtseys to her*]

---

[6] Welcome

[7] Fool

[8] Fool

VILLAGE PEOPLE: Daniya![9] Daniya! Welcome back General! Daniya **ʒiàgàba!**[10]

[*One of the hefty men returns to the stage as Egunnu is about to leave and she stops*]

HEFTY MAN: Ʒiàgàba, should we bury the man? It seems he is dead.

EGUNNU: Where are the others?

HEFTY MAN: They are waiting in the front of your compound for your instructions.

EGUNNU: Do not bury him. Take him to the **Bŏci.**[11] He is a tough breed, and his skull and sinews shall make a very good **Àrùkù,**[12] the medicine for my future victories.

HEFTY MAN: It shall be done Ʒiàgàba.

[*He leaves the stage. Egunnu surveys the milling villagers again*]

EGUNNU: Good-for-nothing geckos.

[*She hisses and saunters off the stage. Curtain closes*]

---

[9] Salutation to a person of high rank
[10] General
[11] Medicine-man
[12] Medicine

SCENE FOUR

The curtain opens to the palace of the Alaafin. He is confabbing with his four generals on the outcome of the battle with the Nupe.

The Alaafin is clad in a thick and patterned cotton dress and a broad leopard skin was knotted like a toga over the cotton flowing gown.

He sits on a carved stool while his four generals, Sunu, Ajangbadi, Eruku-Ina, and Jebata stand before him.

ALAAFIN: The victory we had today was because of Elemoso. We must crush the Nupe.

JEBATA: Kabiyesi, my lord. We must crush the Nupe.

[*The others nod in agreement*]

AJANGBADI: The Nupe must be crushed but our soldiers were heavily wounded and – [*The Alaafin cuts in*]

ALAAFIN: What are you saying? That I must not return to Oyo-Ile? That I must not fulfill the dying wish of my father? What are you saying?

[*The Alaafin is visibly angry, but his generals seem unmoved*]

SUNU: May I speak Kabiyesi?

[*Alaafin motions to him to continue*]

Kabiyesi you are right. We must take back Oyo Ile and remember that my father promised your father when they met for the first time at Ilesa-bariba that these lands will be rid of the Nupe menace.

Their princes have become highway robbers and our traders could no longer walk the roads to bring the abundance of distant lands to our people.

My people of Borgu and your people have a common enemy in the Nupe and that is why I serve you Kabiyesi.

[*As if on cue, Eruku-ina continues*]

ERUKU-INA: Kabiyesi, we owed today's victory to Elemoso, the commander of the king's guards. The Nupe have access to the desert horses and we do not have. But our soldiers were valiant. All we crave is a little rest so that the bleeding wounds of the soldiers may heal, and the hands may be strong again to wield the sword.

[*A servant enters the room, and he stops, gazing fixedly at the Alaafin. The Alaafin motions to him to approach the throne and he moves to whisper to him while the Alaafin nods in agreement. Then the Alaafin addresses the four*]

ALAAFIN: Generals, I have heard your words. You are dismissed for now.

[*As the Generals leave the stage, two men in flowing dresses and balloon-like headdresses, led by the royal bard, enter the stage. They greet the Alaafin with a bow and a clenched fist raised over their heads*]

ROYAL BARD: They have arrived my mighty king, they have come. **Imale**, from the place where shortened grasses meet the teeth of the cattle as the wind blows the trails of the camels away from the desert sands.

Imale, the one who made the lightest of burdens and turned it into a headdress.

They asked Imale, "Why you look askance at the beads of the maidens in the king's market?" He squinted his gaze and grabbed the snake-like bottle. **Imale**![13] You are in the presence of the deity among men.

[*He turns to the Alaafin and knelt*]

Second to none but the gods!

Son of death,

Son of loss,

Son of catastrophe that the Tapa called 'Idagiri'.

Offspring of destruction!

Your ancestors bestrode these lands like a pestilence.

It did not spoil in the time of the one with the shot-out eyes like bitter kola,

It was not wasted at the time of Aganju!

It was kept safely in the days of Orompoto,

It was intact in the days of Ajaka the dread-locked king,

It will not collapse in your time!

---

[13] Yoruba word for Malians or Mandika people who were also Muslims.

[*He turns to the two visitors and as if on cue, they walk six steps to the king and stopped*]

Imale, you are in the presence of the thunder.

TRADERS: Mansoo![14] Mansoo! Your majesty the king!

ALAAFIN: Imale traders you are welcome to my realm. I hope my friend, Askia, is well and in good spirits?

TRADER ONE: He is well Mansoo, He is well, and we bear his greetings and goodwill to you and your realm.

ALAAFIN: Naturally, I should have received you with the lords of my realm like the last time. But I must hasten to consolidate our military advantage over the Nupe.

[*He pauses* and *turns to the royal bard*].

You, get me the Balogun-Parakoyi. I want him here immediately. Time moves like an unstable whirlwind and like the thirst of a lover, it soon spends itself and nothing remains in the morning to tell of the tryst of the night.

So, have you brought what I want?

---

[14] Mandika word for "King"

TRADER TWO: Mansoo, Askia has decided to allow the Wangarawa[15] to bring the horses to your stables. But the lord you told to make trade palaver with us is yet to give us what we can take to the Wangarawa. We have-

[*The Alaafin cuts in as he has become livid with anger*]

ALAAFIN: You mean the Parakoyi has withheld what is due to you?

TRADERS: Mansoo! Mansoo!

[*The royal bard entered the chamber with the Balogun-Parakoyi, a man with a leathery face and who had a single robe tied around his slender body like a toga, following closely behind him*]

BALOGUN-PARAKOYI: Kabiyesi ooo

[*He removes his cap and prostrates himself flatly on the matted ground, turning to the right and the left in his prostrate stance*]

I shift to the right, I shift to the left. May your reign be more glorious than that of your ancestors. May 'ase', the code of authority never stops from your mouth. Kabiyesi ooooh!

ALAAFIN: You may rise.

---

[15] West African Trading Tribe

[*He rises to sit on the matted ground. He nods at the two traders*].

BALOGUN-PARAKOYI: Kabiyesi, you summoned me.

[*As if on cue, the royal bard motions to the traders to come with him, and he leads them away, the three of them walking backwardly until they exit the stage*].

ALAAFIN: While I was waiting for you to arrive, the Imale traders told me that you have not given them what they wanted.

BALOGUN-PARAKOYI: There is no lie in this, Kabiyesi. But I did not willfully withhold our means of exchange, they are the ones who changed songs in the middle of the dance.

ALAAFIN: Open that I may see, give meaning that I may receive understanding.

BALOGUN-PARAKOYI: The royal store does not have enough of the articles of bronze, dried kola-nuts, and woven clothes that we normally use to exchange for the goods of the desert.

The Imale and their Wangarawa friends know that we are in dire conditions, especially with the blockage of the trade routes to the Hausa by the Nupe.

ALAAFIN: But the Imale people are also in pain. Or are they not affected by what is happening to us? They no longer get our goods. It appears that the falling heavens are not the concern of one person.

BALOGUN-PARAKOYI: 'tis true Kabiyesi but our friends knew that the falling heavens will land on us before them. They want to help and profit also. The only exit at the neck of the palm tree that I can see is for us to tarry a bit longer here in Igboho-

ALAAFIN: Agbedo![16] We must not witness it! I have decided to return the Kingdom to Oyo-Ile, the place where my fathers started all things, and nothing shall change it. I swore an oath to my father, that I shall return the capital to Oyo-Ile, and it shall be done. No matter the cost, it shall be done.

BALOGUN-PARAKOYI: Then we must give them what they want.

[*The Alaafin fixes his gaze on Balogun Parakoyi and Parakoyi matches the gaze evenly while the curtain gradually closes*]

---

[16] Impossible!

Scene Five

The curtain opens as the five men were leaving the diviner's house. The diviner's place has about five or six large figurines with baleful eyes, some in kneeling positions, and many aesthetically carved gourds and calabashes. A dying ember at the right corner of the stage glows intermittently as the air blows life to it. The body of Elemoso lies in the center of the stage.

FIVE HEFTY MEN: We take our leave, **Bǒci.** Farewell, **Bǒci.**

DIVINER: People of the same homestead do not bid one another farewell.

[*He turns to look at the body on the floor*]

What should I make of this now?

Egunu would just badger into somebody and make one's house the den of her castaways. What good will this kind of multiple piercings do to anyone in this world?

[*He hisses angrily*]

It would have been many hours since this fellow died.

[*He squats and prods him with his left index finger, and he jumps quickly as if he felt something shocking*]

Is he not dead? This is not possible.

[*He moves briskly to the rafter that is on the top of the dying ember and brings out a tray, places it on the ground, and sits down with his legs elliptically encircling the tray*]

DIVINER: Bring me into your fold and keep me not in the dark spaces. You are the one who said that mysteries of the deities shall be made plain to the child that sucked the breasts of the beaded mothers.

[*He makes patterns on the tray. Slowly, he stands up and the stage gradually darkens, and the light gradually brightens and it focuses on Elemoso standing upright. Slow and eerie drumming of five-beat patterns can be heard in the background.*]

ELEMOSO: The journey of the initiated shall be made through thorns and briars. They asked him to sup with them and mirth filled his heart. In the place of the feast, they gave toads and vinegar to the parched palate. The world of men, the world of monsters! The world of laughter, the world of pestilence, where the sweetness of the honey comes with stings. I must hasten to the place of eternal shadows, to the valley of potsherds, where my father and my mother beckons to me, to come to wait for the next moment of rebirth and forgetfulness. I must hasten-

[*He is interrupted by the diviner, who has joined him on the stage*]

DIVINER: Where are you hastening to? Who told you that you are done with the task of living?

ELEMOSO: I don't know who you are. Or are you sent by the Alaafin to make this journey with me? But no one sojourns with Eso, for Eso is no king and he must walk alone to the place of potsherd. I shall no longer be delayed. I can hear their voices.

[*As he makes to leave, the diviner dives to grab his right leg. The slow drumming continues in the background*]

DIVINER: The water pebble rolled, many revolutions, and a sudden stop when barricaded by the wall of many crevices. Who is the wall if not the witness of destiny, the one who inhabits the here and the there, or the one who gave

gyamã[17] the chameleon the many clothes that were stolen from the owners when the gust visited the habitation of bulrushes?

[*Elemoso strives to be set free from the diviner's firm grip*]

ELEMOSO: What is your concern in this matter old one? Why put a stop to the journey of a man to the labyrinth of many shadows? Let, '**ilepa**[18]', the firm, solid, and caked face of mother earth receive the wasted body of the champion of uncertain provenance. The house of **apaadi**[19] and its undulating floor of glitzy potsherds wait for the son of the compound, and I ask you to let me go my way.

DIVINER: Let truth course from my lips. The matter is of no concern to me in any way, except for the message from **kpàkogi**[20] that your task is unfinished and that you must be stopped from reaching **ekági,**[21] the citadel of the black ants, the keepers of the gates of liminality, where the living and the dead trade spaces.

---

[17] chameleon

[18] The caked dust of the cemetery

[19] Potsherds. The Yoruba believe that the great beyond is tiled with potsherds.

[20] Divination board

[21] Anthill built by black ants. It is believed that the Anthill separates the world of the living from the world of the dead.

ELEMOSO: It is my place to die, I have no other destiny than the one of death that was apportioned to me by my king.

DIVINER: It is the same for all of us, but my fear is for the one that sent me on an errand and not for the one I deliver the message to. Your task is unfinished but I do not know what the task is, and yet I must bring you back from the place of liminality. This I must do, for this is what the gods have willed.

[*Elemoso hisses and strives to break free*]

DIVINER: lá kútí![22] It is from the home I departed, 'tis this path that I traversed,

I arrived, I arrived, and I became the companion of the python,

I sidestepped the arenas where vultures made supper with the eyeballs of the curious,

To reach the clearing in the enchanted forest, where the ghostly elders decided the destiny of the ones who forgot the rites of penitence.

The hornbill visited the crypts, where the bodies of the ones who departed were,

in the morning were laid,

---

[22]Swearing by a masquerade.

Searching for the entrails from the punctured bellies,

But a body was declared unfit for the congress of the carrion eaters,

"Why this body?" I asked.

"Hens shall not eat the entrails of roosters" The reply.

For this, I hasten to catch up with your soul,

Before it reaches the watery curtains of separation,

Where the dead shall no longer converse with the living.

You must tarry to hear what I must say,

For the ear of the mouse cups the footfalls of the cat,

The ear of the mother never misses the cry of the neonate,

You must tarry and wait to hear what I must say.

The elder summon the soul of the bat,

But the youth have the ears of the wandering birds,

You must tarry to hear what I must say,

no feast is too much for the vulture,

no appeasement is too great for the hornbill,

You must tarry and wait to hear what I must say.

To run from ignominy,

The lord of Osile begged the land to open,

The land agreed and allowed him to descend into its bowels.

For this reason, the land became indebted,

and it must vomit what he has swallowed,

What did the land swallow?

He swallowed the carcass of the undead

And he got a swollen abdomen as a testament to its gluttony.

The constipation of the land shall not subside

unless he vomits the thing he swallowed.

What did the land swallow?

He swallowed the carcass of the undead.

It is the gourd that is discarded and never the porcelain,

three is for the initiate, two

is for the novice,

The remnant is for the devotees.

The gong screams when beaten with the rod,

the cudgel by torrential rain makes the wall sullen.

The cat does not join them when bewitchment kills the unfortified.

Albino cannot be obscured in the marketplace.

The gods saw a companion,

But man's derision made them blind.

You have been noticed by the elders,

The ones who woke without hassles-

and struck a friendship with daylight.

You have been told to tarry for a little longer,

You must hear what I have to say.

ELEMOSO: What have you got to say?

DIVINER: Come with me to find out

[*The slow drumming stops, and it becomes gradually dark on both. Slowly another light shines at the left side of the stage and the Diviner is seen squatting and holding the sitting Elemoso, whose back snugly rests comfortably on the wall*]

ELEMOSO: [*coughing loudly*]

DIVINER: You are back, you are well. Be easy with yourself.

ELEMOSO: why[*coughs*] am I here?

DIVINER: You are back among us; you are with us among the living. Your many wounds shall be salved with healing balm and when they close, you shall be inoculated against the blow of steel.

ELEMOSO: Why bring me back?

[*He searchingly examines the Diviner's face. The Diviner points at his abdomen*]

DIVINER: I saw the mark of the crab on you. You are the child of the house. The rules of the novice shall not be binding on the initiate. I was brought to this land, also, as a captive.

[*He shows him the markings on his stomach that form a crab. Egunu enters the stage. She is visibly angry at the sight of Elemoso and the Diviner*]

EGUNU: Bǒci! Why bring back to life that which the gods have accepted into the **sấmã?**[23]

[*She pointed at Elemoso*]

He is not supposed to be living. He is dead.

[*She motions to the two men that are with her*]

Take the Oyo warrior to the dungeon!

DIVINER: I did not bring him back. The gods did.

Curtain Closes.

---

[23] sky

ACT TWO

SCENE ONE

The curtain opens to the funeral scene. There are five men and four women on the stage when the curtain opens. Two out of the men wrap a wooden effigy with a broad sheet of woven jute. Two other men prepare a platform, apparently to place the wrapped wooden effigy on it.

The generals, Sunu, Ajangbadi, Eruku-Ina, and Jebata arrive on the scene. Jebata nods in approval as the four men placed the wrapped wood on the prepared platform.

After this, everyone kneels before the platform. There is slow and mournful drumming in the background.

JEBATA: It is when we die that we become statues. The time has come, dear friend and comrade. The time has come that we send you to the place where you shall be gathered with our fathers.

SUNU, AJANGBADI and ERUKU-INA: Yes, it is time.

JEBATA: The obsequies of the warrior shall not be uneventful like the one of the stray dog.

SUNU, AJANGBADI, and ERUKU-INA: Not like a stray dog.

JEBATA: The battle became hot, and our men despaired when the calvary of the Tapa charged. We have worn death like a second skin and waited for its arrival. But the hoofs of their many horses shifted the ground from the feet of the infantry and the falcon failed to hear the call of the falconer.

SUNU, AJANGBADI and ERUKU-INA: Yes, it is true.

JEBATA: Fright led to the flight and the men went in different directions.

SUNU, AJANGBADI, and ERUKU-INA: There is no lie in this.

JEBATA: But you stood because you, Eso, are the protector of the realm. The protector does not take the barbed point of the arrow in the back but in the front with his bare chest. For if the protector is found dead with a stab in the back, he did not fall from treacherous hands but from the consequences of fright.

SUNU, AJANGBADI and ERUKU-INA: Abomination! The protector shall not take an arrow in the back.

[*The four women started to sing a hymn and the drum increased a little bit in volume*]

CHORUS: Let him pass at this time,

All he craves, beddings of dreams,

Let him pass at this time,

He paid the full price.

JEBATA: Elemoso! Elemoso! You stood and accepted the volley of barbed steel. Death and pestilence and your courage made them seek new habitations.

You turned the tide of the battle, and you stole victory from the jugular of the enemy.

You kept the oath made to your king that even your death shall not make this land unfree. A thousand arrows turned you into a porcupine and the enemy saw your grin instead of self-pity.

[M*ore drumming*]

CHORUS: Let him pass at this time,

All he craves, beddings of dreams,

Let him pass at this time,

He paid the full price.

SUNU: Eso! Till the indeterminate. Till we walk to never meet again.

You confronted the enemy in their thousands, and you transformed, you became a deity, the one with the gods.

CHORUS: Let him pass at this time,

All he craves, beddings of dreams,

Let him pass at this time,

He paid the full price.

[*The men lift the wrapped effigy*]

AJANGBADI: People at the fore, accept him. He is now one of you. People on the aft, give him up because he has changed position.

ERUKU-INA: If the owner of the front yard does not die, his front yard is not overgrown by weeds. We shall keep your yard clean and creeping animals shall not turn the house of the mighty into a habitation.

Farewell, dear comrade, and find rest in the havens of the deities. Eat with them whatever they eat, drink with them whatever they drink. Farewell, farewell, dear friend.

CHORUS: Let him pass at this time,

All he craves, beddings of dreams,

Let him pass at this time,

He paid the full price.

[*They all exit the stage, with the other four men carrying away the effigy. The drumming gradually subsides as the curtain closes*]

SCENE TWO

The stage opens with a young lad being told to go fetch the midwife by an older man. A pregnant woman is standing and swaying, apparently in the early throes of childbirth.

MALAOLU: Ajayi, go fetch Mama Ajiun. Tell her that Moluyi's time has come. Hurry and return to this place.

[*The lad moves speedily from the stage, while the man turns to the pregnant woman*]

Moluyi my child, you will be safe. Mama Ajiun is on the way.

You have walked the right paths and have plucked the leaves of easy birthing. Just like the autumn leaves that are parted from the tree with ease, your child will come out of your womb with ease.

[*Ajiun enters the stage. She has a single patterned cloth wrapped around her chest up her ankle. The lad carries a tote bag, walking closely behind her*]

AJIUN: Has the owner of the house given space?

MALAOLU: Let the visitor have the space.

[*He prostates on sighting Ajiun*].

Ajiun our mother, I thank you for coming. What can we do without you in Aribisasi?

AJIUN: Moluyi, you will give birth to your child. We shall hear the voice of the mother and the cry of the child.

As I was coming from home, I appealed to all mothers of the earth and the ones who are awake in heaven to assemble here with us.

I have given Kola-nut to those who deserve it and evil shall be pushed away. Let all fears perish inside you.

[*She turns to Malaolu who has risen*]

Have you prepared the enclosure?

OLDER MAN: I have done it, our mother.

[*He points to a cube-like enclosure that has a cloth covering all sides at the right side of the stage. Ajiun nods in approval*]

AJIUN: You have done the right thing.

[*She holds Moluyi by the waist and leads her to the enclosure*]

Come with me, my child.

MOLUYI: Mother, this moment has refused to change for me.

AJIUN: It shall soon be sent to the place of forgetfulness.

[*They enter the enclosure. Malaolu paces about while AJIUN can be heard speaking inside the enclosure*].

I beseech you, dear mothers, Moluyi is your daughter and her day of kneeling to receive goodness has arrived. It is a life we ask for. Life for the mother and life for the child.

My mothers, the one who inhabits the earthenware to seek friendship with water, you are the enormous fish that troubles the depths of the ocean.

It is the nondescript utensil that is gobbled by the unstable waters of life, Moluyi is your child and she must not be drowned by the waters of existence.

The rooster that will crow shall not become the food of the hawk when it was a cockerel. Moluyi! It is time.

The fish uses the head to traverse the sea, your child uses the head to emerge from the dark protrusion into our world of light. She is coming. Let your grunt be greater than the pig's and push your child into existence.

[*Moluyi grunts loudly*]

Welcome my child, the world is sweet.

[*The baby cries*].

Behold your child, Moluyi! Moluyi you have entered the place of danger and have emerged unscathed.

[*Ajiun emerges from the enclosure, holding a calabash*]

AJIUN: The mother speaks and the baby cries. Why shall we not rejoice?

[*The man jumps with happiness*].

OLDER MAN: Orisa of the skies I thank you. My ancestors, I thank you. I give thanks to Osun, our mother!

AJIUN: Now take this from me

[*She hands over the calabash*].

We have gotten the goodness, which is the child. This is the placenta, the one the elders call the evil one. Go and bury it and throughout the life of the child, evil shall not know her place of abode.

OLDER MAN: Ase!

[*At that moment, noise can be heard, and two women and two men run from one end of the stage to the other*]

AJIUN: Why are you running? What is happening?

[*She calls out after them*]

RUNNERS: It is the warriors. They have brought war to the village! They have brought war to the village.

[*The stage darkens, and the curtain closes briefly. The curtain opens to a scene of chaos, accompanied by fast-paced martial drumming. Women, children, young men, and old people run helter-skelter on the stage, as they were overpowered and bound by soldiers. With the soldiers are Sunu and Balogun-Parakoyi. Ajiun enters the stage, stops, and surveys the scene.*]

AJIUN: I am Ajiun, the needle that the rooster dares not swallow. Who is that foolish dog that dares to show faces in the courtyard of the Lion? Who dares lead marauding soldiers to the place where warriors dread?

SUNU: Old woman, we are here to do the Alaafin's business. Ọba[24] sent one on an errand and the unbridged Ọbà[25] River has flooded its banks, the Ọba business must be done and the Ọbà River cannot be forded. But I chose to ford this river which happens to be your village.

AJIUN: [*guttural laughter*] You dare come to my village to turn the free into bondmen?

[L*aughter again and the soldiers bring the last of the bound people to the seated group in front of Balogun-Parakoyi who examines them*]

SUNU: What has the world become? A mere woman? That let out urine from the rear. What has - [*Ajiun cuts in*]

AJIUN: Let your mouth be sealed! It is not knowing how to refuse certain errands that made the ladle dip its head inside the hot soup. When one is given the task of a slave, he performs it like the son of the house. But you have chosen to be foolish, and your foolishness shall see you to your grave.

---

[24] King

[25] River Ọbà.

SUNU: Put that way old woman for it is not for me! I intended to spare you for it is the initiate that assists his fellow initiates; because if the initiative fails to help his fellow initiate, the oath of allegiance shall be shamed, and the bind shall be torn. But now I no longer have any scruples and you shall become one of the captives.

[*He motions to a soldier*]

Taker her! Bind her!

[*The soldiers run towards her but with the motion of her hand she stops them*]

AJIUN: Abomination! We shall not hear of the death of Elédùmarè, èèwọ̀ òrìṣà!

[*Balogun-Parakoyi steps away from the captives he was inspecting to confront Sunu*]

BALOGUN-PARAKOYI: What is all this Sunu? Why the haggling and banter over goods that have been already sold?

[*Ajiun steps into the middle of Sunu and Parakoyi*]

AJIUN: It is for the day of trouble that I attended the feasts of the terrestrial mothers, who made mincemeat from the livers of scoundrels like you. It is because of tribulations that I paid my dues at the hills of Aribigba, the only place where the citadels of heaven and the earth share walls.

[*She faces Balogun-Parakoyi*]

Did you not know? Have you not found out that this village is called 'Aribisasi', the place of refuge of the freeborn? Where, by the mandates of the entire deities of Ile-Ife, it shall not be entered by slaves like you?

BALOGUN-PARAKOYI: Sunu! Are you also sleeping like the soldiers? Are you also bewitched? Do your work right now!

SUNU: My consciousness returns from the place of mystery!

[*He moves closer to his hypnotized men and blew a white substance from the small gourd he brings out in a small pouch he carries*]

Come back to life! There is work to be done!

[*The men snap out of their reverie*]

AJIUN: Scoundrels! Do you know whose village you have come to war with? Do you know that this is the birthplace of Elemoso, the one who uses the occiputs of enemies for holding snuffs?

[*Sunu motions to the soldiers to grab her*]

SUNU: As if we do not know already? Seize her!

[*The men encircle her and overpower her*]

AJIUN: [*while struggling to be free*] You will regret your actions today! I am the mother of Elemoso and it is his village that you have made desolate. You will regret this! I promise you!

[*She is tied with others and the soldiers lead the captives out of the stage*]

SUNU: Elemoso is dead. If he was crawling, he would have reached **Alakeji**[26] by now.

BALOGUN-PARAKOYI: Let us make haste. The Imale traders have arrived with the horses that we need. The exchange must be made before nightfall.

[*Sunu surveys the stage briefly and runs off to catch up with the others*]

Curtain closes

---

[26] Another word for the great beyond.

SCENE THREE

The stage opens to a scene of the dungeon with prisoners peeping out from the openings in the wooden doors. A warder leads Elemoso, in chains, out of one of the cells.

WARDER: Oyo move. You are going to **Tunga,**[27] where you will work on the farm and be fed lettuce. No more warring for you. Move!

[*Elemoso moves a few steps and falls flat on the floor*]

WARDER: Oyo falls! Like your slippery people, you are no good to anybody.

[*He stands over him*].

Egunu will not listen. These wounds are yet unhealed.

[27] A settlement where slaves and prisoners are put to work.

[*He bends to pull him up*]

Oyo, stand up.

[*Immediately Elemoso, twists and turns around, grip the warder's left hand with his two hands clenched in chains, pulls up his legs and knees to his chin, and drives both of his loosely tied feet into the chest of the warder. The prisoners in the cells started laughing*]

WARDER: Oyo! Haahhhhhh! Oyo! You are dead!

ELEMOSO: Not today [*He brings him to the ground, twists, and slams his body over him*]

WARDER: O—yo

[*Elemoso's hands had found his windpipe as he bears on him, both struggling*]

ELEMOSO: It is for a day like this that I became an initiate of the cult of leopards. So that my back shall not know the ground, I supped with the largest cats. 'I rise, I rise' says Akata the panther in the hills of the morning dew.

[*The warder stops struggling. Elemoso searches in his robes and brings out a curved rod. He uses the rod to undo the clasp of chains on his legs. A prisoner beckons to him*]

PRISONER: Come let me remove the chains from your hands.

[*He hands the rod to him, and the prisoner inserts the rod into the shackles, and it falls to the ground. Elemoso makes to leave but he stops and returns to the cells*]

ELEMOSO: If freedom is what you desire, the gates to freedom are opened unto you.

[*He opens all the cells, and he walks briskly away from the dungeon. It is dark and a few seconds later, the light opens on Elemoso near Egunu's horse*]

ELEMOSO: [*As he unties the horse, he speaks to it*]

Hear my words, dear friend. I know you must be tired. But you brought me here and you shall have the honor of taking me back.

[*He mounts the horse. At the same time, the voice of the warder can be heard*]

WARDER'S VOICE: Gãgwa![28] Gãgwa! Oyo has escaped! Oyo has escaped!

ELEMOSO: Hiya! Let's go! Hiya!

[*The stage darkens as he rides on the horse. The light opens on Egunnu and some soldiers*]

EGUNNU: He must not escape. He must be captured dead or alive. He is the most important

[28] Escape!

soldier of the Alaafin, and he has seen our defences. Move!

[*The Soldiers run, leaving Egunu standing and staring at the Audience*]

EGUNU: I went on a hunting expedition, and I returned with the hefty buffalo. I relished the prospect of an evening meal of roasted and tender bovine, but my animal had found life and sauntered out of captivity! Hahhh blood will flow! Hahh heads will roll!

Curtain Closes.

SCENE FOUR

The curtain opens on Elemoso.

The stage shows desolation. Pestles and brooms are in different places, stools are upside down.

[*Elemoso dismounts*]

ELEMOSO: Has the owner of the house given space?

[*Silence answers him*]

ELEMOSO: Who is in this village of Aribisasi? Ajiun my mother, where are you? Has the owner of the house yielded space?

[*Silence answers him again*]

ELEMOSO: Has war overtaken this village? Has pestilence taken them? If it is pestilence, where are the carcasses of the bodies wasted by diseases?

No, it must have been war. War has entered the sacred spaces. War knows no boundary and it does not spare the habitat of the brave.

War entered Aribisasi and has taken Ajiun, the mother of Elemoso. Hahhhhh!

[*Malaolu who was with Moluyi enters the stage. Elemoso turns to face him*]

ELEMOSO: Who are you?

MALAOLU: Eso, I am the one left as a father to Moluyi, the daughter of Iya-Alaro the indigo seller, and your mother's sister.

ELEMOSO: Where is everybody?

MALAOLU: We have been ravished by the ones we trust, plundered at midday by the ones who swore to be our protector.

War entered Aribisasi but the faces that came to war were known faces and because of that, we left our matchets hanging on the rafters.

ELEMOSO: Your words are many but the facts are few.

MALAOLU: The soldiers of Alaafin invaded us and carried many of us away as slaves. They were led by Balogun-Parakoyi and Sunu, the Bariba warrior who fights for the Alaafin.

ELEMOSO: But I heard that hens do not eat the entrails of other hens and roosters stay away from the carrion of another rooster?

MALAOLU: The world has turned upside down, Eso. Even pigeons do not discriminate in their meals.

ELEMOSO: Are you the only one that survived?

MALAOLU: There are others in the bush.

ELEMOSO: Go and bring them here. I want everyone to stand before me.

[Malaolu leaves the stage. Elemoso paces on the stage as he soliloquizes]

ELEMOSO: Ibosi ooooooooo![29] The world has gone topsy-turvy. The sacred places have vanished, and the oases have become patched lands. **Ibosi ooooooooo!**

Avarice enters the town in the company of gluttony.

Nothing was left standing and everything good, the ones that please the eye, and the ones that are sweet on the palate, all were torched, pushed into the rapines.

---

[29] Calling attention of others to a misdeed.

[*He stops and gazes at the audience as if in a trance*].

Ajiun my mother. The owner of Agate Beads. I had gone to the farm to find the yams of the previous year; I had gone to the brook to find the first waters of the dawn. I returned home but no one answered my salutations.

Ajiun, return to me. Men of the world are wicked; they are full of bile and hate. Who would have thought that the same water that nourishes the fish would conspire with fire to cook the same fish?

Had I known that the world is a field of battle, a theatre of unceasing conflict, I would have started my training earlier.

I would have braced myself since childhood and made the houses of the warmongers my place of habitation.

The world is an unceasing battle and even in death, rest is elusive.

[*Malaolu leads men, women, and young children to the stage. Moluyi is with them too with a baby strapped to her back*]

MALAOLU: We are all here. The remnant of Aribisasi. We are all here, we are no more than this.

[*Elemoso surveys all of them*]

ELEMOSO: Those who have been plundered must survive by becoming bandits themselves. It is the wickedness of men that makes the meek to do the charm of the impenetrability of the steel to his body. There is no time for brooding over your condition. Let every man get his sword or matchet. Today we become outlaws.

This day, we become scoundrels. We are no longer under any master and no king shall accept our curtseys.

This day we become deaths, the marauders of the highway, the vermin of the countryside, the commanders-in-chief of pestilence. We are free!

[*They reply to him in unison*]

EVERYONE: Hey!

ELEMOSO: [*He motions to Malaolu*]

Old one, bring me Esu, the god of the crossroads. I have a message to send him.

[*Malalolu leaves to fetch the effigy of Esu. Elemoso continues*]

Freedom comes at the hour of death. I dined daily with death as I pledged my loyalty to Alaafin of Oyo. But who is that treacherous person that sends destruction to the homestead of the dutiful servant?

EVERYONE: Only the bush rat!

ELEMOSO: Oh bush-rat, is this your character? you drank the land and made a covenant with the deity of the oracle. Is this your character? Oh, bush-rat? We thought we stood on the same land. The same land where we ate rodents? The same land received commands from the heavens and declared us free of death.

[*He turns to look vacantly at the Audience*]

My king, I entered the chambers in the abyss of the underworld, and in nakedness, I pledged my sword to you.

[*He hisses loudly*]

This is not what we agreed upon.

[*Malaolu arrives, carrying the effigy of Esu. He sets it down before Elemoso*]

ELEMOSO: Esu laaroye the stone-wall. The one who entangles the idle in unwanted trouble.

Esu, the one who stoned the ram. Esu I beseech you. You have no knees for supplication.

Esu Laaroye, the one who has clothes but dispossesses others of their apparel. Laaroye!

They mourn but you shed blood as tears, they defecate but you bring out intestines. Laaroye! the man of the external realms, the owner of the downtown hamlet.

Esu Laalu, the mourner-in-chief, scares the bereaved with his tears of blood. Laaroye I have come to you. Your ointment is the red oil of the palm, but it is the Oyo who asked me to give you what you despised most and that is the thick oil of palm nut.

[He *places the whitish ointment which is the thick oil of palm nut on the figurine. Then he kneels*]

Far from it, my father. I did not bring the thick oil of palm nut to you. It is the work of Oyo. So, go to them and turn their homestead into a place of desolation. Put them asunder for they have done the abominable.

Esu Laalu! The moment has come for you to fight.

[*He rises and addresses the congregation*]

The matter is settled. It is time for vengeance!

EVERYONE: HEY!! It is time for war,
He that the war finds,
Death without consequences.
It is time for war,
He that the war finds,
Death without consequences.

[*Dancing and drumming till fade. Curtain closes*]

SCENE FIVE

The curtain opens to a scene of men and women carrying baskets of produce on their heads. The background depicts short trees and shrubs, suggesting derived savannah. They had not moved more than three steps when Elemoso and his people run to the stage to accost them.

ELEMOSO: Stop! No one must move a step

further. [*The basket carriers stop*].

Who are you and where are you heading to?

[*One of the women steps forward*]

IDOWU: My lord, I am Idowu, and I am the leader of the traders of Alaafin. We are going to the headwaters of Oya River, a three day journey to exchange these Kolanuts [*She points at the baskets*] for the goods of the desert.

Can we continue our journey?

ELEMOSO: [*Guttural laughter*]

You cannot continue.

[*He motions to his matchet-wielding men*].

The master of the slave is the owner of the goods. Seize them all!

[*They pounce on them*]

IDOWU: My lord, have mercy! We are on the king's business! Have mercy, my lord! Have mer-

[*Strong hands lift her and throw her to the ground. She is tied with ropes, as well as others*]

ELEMOSO: We are the lords of these lands. No king rules us.

[*The traders wail as they follow Elemoso and his soldiers away from the stage, tied together at the waist, with baskets balanced on their heads.*]

Curtain closes

SCENE SIX

The scene is the Palace of the Alaafin. The Generals, Jebata, Eruku-Ina, Sunu, and Ajagbandi, and the minister of trade, Balogun-Parakoyi are sitting on the mat.

[*The Alaafin appears and the five prostrate in greeting.*]

JEBATA, ERUKU-INA, AJANGBADI, SUNU, BALOGUN: Kabiyesi ooooooooooooooooooooo!

[*The Alaafin takes his seat on the carved wooden stool*]

ALAAFIN: What is it that I am hearing? Are bandits attacking our trades' people on their way to the savannah? Who is behind this? Is it the Nupe again? Or your people the Bariba.

[*Looking pointedly at Jebata*]

JEBATA: Kabiyesi, it is not my people, and it is not the Nupe also.

ALAAFIN: Then who is it? It did not spoil in the time of my father, Ofinran and it must not spoil in my own time. Who is it?

SUNU: Kabiyesi, one of the traders that escaped told us that it was Elemoso who led the bandits that waylaid them.

ALAAFIN: Elemoso? But he is dead. The dead do not converse with the living. Elemoso is dead.

ERUKU-INA: Apparently he is still alive. We must not forget that Elemoso is powerful and well-fortified by the gods.

BALOGUN-PARAKOYI: This is the fiftieth attack on our caravan, Kabiyesi. The last trade mission that we sent was supposed to bring back the much-needed rock salt. Now we shall lack salt in our foods for the next three moons.

ALAAFIN: But Elemoso is my loyal servant who swore to me that he would never betray me. Why has he become a turncoat? Why is he fighting us?

[*Jebata gave Sunu a knowing look*]

SUNU: Jebata why are you looking at me as if I am some culprit? You should be directing your query to Balogun-Parakoyi. He was the one who-

[*Balogun-Parakoyi interrupts him*]

BALOGUN-PARAKOYI: Let it hang in your mouth you Bariba scum. You must never- [*Alaafin cuts in*]

ALAAFIN: Is it in my presence that all of you are haggling like traders that failed to reach a bargain? [*All of them prostrate.*]

JEBATA, ERUKU-INA, AJANGBADI, SUNU, BALOGUN: Kabiyesi oooooooooooooooooooo!

ALAAFIN: Balogun, speak. Tell me what happened.

BALOGUN: Kabiyesi, after you gave us the order to find all means to pay the Imale traders and we did not have enough kola nuts to pay them for the horses, I decided to harvest people from Aribisasi village to make up for the shortfall. Sunu and his soldiers followed me to raid the village.

ALAAFIN: But that village is owned by Elemoso.

BALOGUN: Your order must be carried out Kabiyesi. You ordered that- [*Alaafin cuts in*]

ALAAFIN: I know what I ordered. I am the king and I have no remorse. I perch above all because I take what is mine.

JEBATA, ERUKU-INA, AJANGBADI, SUNU, BALOGUN: Kabiyesi oooooooooooooooooooo!

ALAAFIN: Elemoso knows the consequences of revolting against me. He has done the sacrilegious and he must face the consequences.

[*He rises and others rise with him*].

Bring his head to me. Elemoso must die!

JEBATA, ERUKU-INA, AJANGBADI, SUNU, BALOGUN: Kabiyesi oooooooooooooooooooo!

Curtain closes

ACT THREE

Scene One

The stage opens to an angry scene in the palace of Elente, the King of the Nupe. Several chiefs were seated on the floor in front of the King. Egunu and a male General stand before the king.

ELENTE: I am no longer interested in capturing the escaped Oyo soldier. I want to finish the conquest of Oyo. I can no longer tolerate the existence of the Alaafin in the part of the world that he inhabits.

CHIEFS: Sàmăzagudù[30] Elente! May your reign be long.

[30] Salutation to the Elente.

EGUNU: Your Majesty, I am ashamed that the Oyo escaped from my keep. Allow me to redeem myself and let me lead the invasion of Oyo-Igboho, the new abode of the Alaafin. Allow me, my lord.

ELENTE: What do you say to this Ndăèjì**?**

[*Elente asks the chief on his right*]

NDAEJI: Your Majesty, the job of emptying the bowels is too important to be given to a maid, Egunu should not be allowed to lead the invasion of Oyo.

[*Other Chiefs concur*]

CHIEFS: You have spoken well, ã[31], you have spoken well.

EGUNU: [*looking menacingly at Elente*]

The banana tree shaded dĩnci,[32] the black plum tree when it was young but on reaching maturity, it became an obstruction to the plum tree farmer. I got you here and you-

[*Ndăèji cuts in*]

---

[31] Yes.

[32] Black plum tree.

NDAEJI: You shall not address the Elente as if he is still your sibling! You will show respect!

[*Egunu instantly bows*]

EGUNU: Forgive me, your majesty.

NDAEJI: Your majesty! have mercy on her, she needs to be reminded that she has not stopped having **áyíla**[33]

[*Everyone laughs and Egunu leaves the stage angrily*]

ELENTE: [*Addressing the male general*]

Ùbandawaki!

UBANDAWAKI: Your majesty

[*Answers with the right clenched fist raised*]

ELENTE: You shall gather the calvary, the dàkarè,[34], and a third of the palace guards at dawn and bring the Alaafin to my palace in chains.

UBANDAWAKI: It is done, your majesty.

[*Curtseys with the right clenched fist raised*]

---

[33] Monthly menstrual flow.

[34] infantry

ELENTE: The council is now dismissed.

CHIEFS: Sàmãzagudù Elente! Long may you reign.

Curtain closes

SCENE TWO

The stage opens to the scene of Oyo soldiers matching behind Sunu. A fast-paced but low-volume martial drumming can be heard in the background.

From the opposite side of the stage, Elemoso emerges at the head of his soldiers. Images of short trees and shrubs provide verisimilitude of derived savannah.

SUNU: Stop right there! The morning has broken on you. The wind has blown, and the anus of the hen has been exposed. Light has exposed the face of the one that used the cover of the dark to do evil. Elemoso-

[*Elemoso interrupts him*]

ELEMOSO: Seal your lying mouth. If treachery has another name, that name is Sunu. We postponed the arrest of the thief; the thief became emboldened and arrested the farm owner.

SUNU: I have not come to exchange words with you, old friend. It is the Alaafin that wants your head brought to him before eventide. They told you not to cook the stew of fear, you cooked the stew of fear. They told you not to come through the backyard, you came through the backyard.

You have eaten the abominable and your eyes shall see death. Elemoso!

[*At the mention of Elemoso's name, the soldiers that are with Sunu started to talk loudly among themselves*]

ELEMOSO: That is me! You have summoned the strong man. Two hundred animals of the wild cannot ambush the panther.

[H*e points at Sunu's soldiers*]

Why the screech like a troop of monkeys?

The only word allowed to the pig is the grunt, and many grunts shall remain sealed in the belly, never to be uttered and never to be vocalized.

[*A third of the soldiers leaves Sunu and moves toward Elemoso. Elemoso's soldiers charge toward them*]

SUNU'S SOLDIERS: Elemoso has become Orisa! Elemoso has become Orisa! Elemoso has become Orisa!

[*A few spaces from Elemoso, they all prostrate.*]

ELEMOSO: Sunu, see what has become of your army? Are you sure you will not join them to pay obeisance to the king of the wastelands?

I am Eso, the one who stops the shower of arrows with a bare chest and never in the back. I am the apparition who returned from the market-day obsequies to finish the undone task.

[*Sunu motions to one of the soldiers that are still with him. The soldier leaves the stage*]

SUNU: Elemoso, I know the path and I know the valley. I know that it is only the dog that enters the den of the lion without expecting to be bathed in its blood. I came to you prepared.

[*The soldier returns with Ajiun, Elemoso's mother in chains*]

ELEMOSO: Iya mi! My mother! Ajiun my mother?

SUNU: I came to you well prepared. I saved the best for the last. I shall spare your mother's life, but the price shall be your own life. Your life for her own life.

ELEMOSO: [*Addressing his mother*]

Ajiun my mother.

AJIUN: Eso the beloved of the deities, I should be happy that my eyes see you again. What is coming out of my mouth? I am very happy. The cause of my sadness is that the scoundrels rule and the world no longer has a place of refuge.

ELEMOSO: Sweet is the milk of the breast of the mother, life courses through it and I hung to it.

Ajiun my mother, existence has dealt with us unfairly and all we have ever known is bitterness greater than that of the bitter leaf. My mother, wait here and let me depart before you. For you must return to Aribisasi.

[*She turns to Sunu*]

AJIUN: Will you not allow me to embrace my son for the last time on this side?

[*He does not answer her*]

Let me embrace my son before he dies.

[*Elemoso steps forward, throwing away his weapons as he moves towards his mother and Sunu. Sunu motions to a soldier to remove Ajiun's chains*]

ELEMOSO: Mother, my mother.

[*As he is a few steps away from Ajiun, she dips her hand into her front orifice and brings a very small gourd, laughing loudly at Elemoso. Elemoso runs towards her shouting*].

No! Nooooooooooooooooooooooooooooooooo!

[*The soldier tries to snatch the gourd from Ajiun, but Elemoso collapses into her while Ajiun throws the gourd into her mouth, chewing and swallowing fast*]

SUNU: [*Moving speedily to them*]

What is happening here?

[*Ajiun grips Elemoso, smiling, contorting as she foams in the mouth*]

ELEMOSO: Mother, but I told you to let me go before you? Why?

[*Sunu commands the soldiers*]

SUNU: Today's battle is over. Seize Elemoso!

[*As Elemoso was being pulled up from the ground, the sound of the neighing of horses and drumming can be heard in the background. A scout runs to the stage*]

SCOUT: Nupe soldiers are here! The Nupe has arrived!

SOLDIERS: [*shouting at the same time and moving about the stage in confusion*]

Nupe oooo! Tapa[35] ooooh! Nupe ooooh! Tapa oooooh!

[*The stage becomes dark briefly and the light gradually shines on Elemoso, standing with a dark-skinned man, clad in a red and black robe*]

ELEMOSO: Esu laaroye, why are you here? Why are you here?

ESU: The one who defecates forgets but the one who packs it will always be reminded by the stench. The errand you sent me is what I have come to deliver.

You told me to turn Oyo upside down and wrought upon it the type of deed that the python does to its prey. Now Oyo has been driven into the entrapment of Nupe.

Today, Oyo shall become a wasteland and its people shall be carried into captivity.

[*At that moment, Ajiun, Elemoso's mother walks briskly, away from the stage, paying no attention to the two*]

ELEMOSO: [*Tries to run after her but stops in his tracks and turns to Esu*]

My mother's soul is on the way to the Hill of Bayero.

---

[35] Word used by Yoruba when referring to Nupe.

ESU: Yes, she has done what a mother should do.

ELEMOSO: Esu, your task is done. I know I told you that I want Oyo destroyed totally. But my mother is dead and my oath of fealty to Oyo still courses through my veins. It calls me to go lay down my life and defend her.

For Oyo is the husband and I am the bride. I have no other existence than the one Oyo throws at me.

ESU: No one calls for the help of a deity and bars it from doing the task it was summoned to do.

ELEMOSO: Thrice I retreated to Offa and what I do shall not be questioned. I became the spells that I may not be enchanted.

ESU: Let those in the front relieve it, let those at the rear receive it.

[*He brings out the thick oil of the palm nut*]

ELEMOSO: Not this time Esu. Not this time. It is not Oyo that gave you the thick oil of the palm nut.

ESU: Then who did?

[*Esu charges menacingly at him*]

ELEMOSO: I did. **Oferegege!**[36]

[*The stage becomes dark.*]

Curtain closes

[36] The spell uttered to facilitate teleportation.

SCENE THREE

The stage opens to the scene where Sunu and the soldiers of Oyo were shouting Nupe! The Nupe soldiers, with Ubandawaki leading, enter the stage from the left side. There is fast-paced martial drumming in the background.

UBANDAWAKI: Sunu the Bariba, a soldier of fortune is always in search of new masters after losing the previous battle. You will die today.

SUNU: Hear foolish talks from Tapa. My death shall witness unceasing adjournment while yours shall happen today.

[*At that moment, Elemoso enters the stage and runs and slams himself into Ubandawaki*]

ELEMOSO: Oyo it is time to die!

SOLDIERS: Elemosooooooooooooooooo!

[*They follow him, and the stage becomes a cacophony of fighting and shouting. Gradually the light dims until it becomes dark briefly. The noise also gradually reduces until it becomes silent. The light returns. Many soldiers are lying on the stage. Sunu surveys the scene. Alaafin arrives with Jebata, Eruku-Ina, Ajangbadi.*]

SUNU: [*Raises left clenched fist*] Kabiyesi oooooh!

ALAAFIN: I got the word that the Nupe army is on the way to attack us in Igboho. I decided to lead the generals to meet them.

SUNU: My lord, though I lost all the men that rode with me in the morning, the battle has been won.

ALAAFIN: The battle has been won? How?

SUNU: My lord, Elemoso

[*Pointing towards the body of Elemoso on the ground among other soldiers*]

Eso did what his fathers have always done. He charged into the enemy and his bravery maddened the soldiers. They all died laughing like hyenas.

ALAAFIN: Is this the last we shall see of the Nupe?

JEBATA: It seems so my lord. The Nupe's army has been defeated totally in this war and it will take three seasons before they can recover from this defeat. Should we march to their capital city?

ALAAFIN: That is not my preoccupation. My desire, right now, is to fulfill the pledge I made to my father that I shall return to Oyo-Ile after the Nupe has been defeated. Today I shall fulfill that pledge.

[*They all salute with clenched fists*]

JEBATA, SUNU, ERUKU-INA, AJANGBADI: Kabiyesi oooooooooo!

ALAAFIN: Jebata, as of today you have become the Iba Oshorun.[37] You will rule with me in the capital city and appease the heavens and my ancestors.

JEBATA: Kabiyesi oooooooo!

[*He salutes with clenched fist*]

ALAAFIN: Soun or Sunu, you should settle in the old Aribisasi, from there you will secure the approach to Oyo-Ile against the Nupe and other enemies of the kingdom. You shall be doing this side and I shall be doing my own at Oyo-Ile.

---

[37] Prime minister.

SUNU: Kabiyesi oooooooooooooooooooooo!! What about Elemoso?

ALAAFIN: What about him? You shall take with you the head of Elemoso and bury it at the entrance of the Aribisasi and no one shall whisper his name. His story shall not be heard again, so that we are not called traitors by the people.

JEBATA, SUNU, ERUKU-INA, AJANGBADI: Kabiyesi oooooooooo!

ALAAFIN: It is time to depart. Four Kings ruled in Igboho, but today I return to the city of my fathers.

[*They all exit the stage, all following the Alaafin. The stage becomes dark briefly and the light returns. Malaolu stands alone on the stage. There is slow drumming. He addresses the audience in an aside*]

MALAOLU: They told us to keep sealed lips on the exploits of Elemoso. No, we shall not do that. Who is Elemoso? Who is Eso?

Eso, the sentinel of Ikoyi, A soldier by day, a robber at nightfall. They spit violence from seven angular points of Ikoyi, And I know all seven.

Those who stand akimbo shall be sent to the war front, those with only kitchen knives shall not be spared from the battle scene, and those with nothing but charms shall be in the company of warriors.

When the archers maintained the frontlines,

The musketeers shall follow closely behind,

The wielders of bludgeons in the middle, and Swordsmen, like the tail of the cobra, at the end of the formation.

Ikoyi Eso, the sentinel, the one who meets death with a grin, The son of 'I did not retreat on the day of the hottest battle.' 'I slept without care when I heard the shouts of heaven.' The mastiff-headed man whose molars crush stones. Ikoyi Eso, the stinger that starts the fight.

I was enthralled by Eso's unceasing warring, But I've had enough of daily conflagrations at Igbon.

One set out for battle with stratagems, another set out for war with deep thoughts, Okotonpori set out for war in a state of anger.

Seventy makes the cohort of Eso at Igbon the capital city, but war reduced them to fifty! Some perished inside the house, some died in the courtyards, and some are still not found to this day.

Eso Ikoyi! You do not take bowshots in the back, for your fathers confronted the volley of arrows with bare chests. Son of the unmourned dead, scion of lonely sleep, Descendant of one who died in armor, For the mastiff-head man dies head and tail.

Offspring of the loader of tiring loot. The battle was fierce, in the phalanx of Eso a few were missing. The battle was tough, Eso dare not call each other by their names. The enemy gains on me and the river is flooded across the banks, but rather than drown in the river, Eso shall fight to the death.

The women of Ikoyi dare not do the craft of basketry. For if they do the craft of basketry, all they have done is remind their lords of the need for war.

The son of the artful archer, who with one bowshot killed six. The seventh gasped and desired death, But Eso Ikoyi disagreed and told him to go, instead, to his father's abode and tell him that he saw the son of the brave at the scene of the battle.

Eso, you are the worthy one, the one who promises death to stifle warfare. Ikoyi Eso was never caught unprepared by war. Ikoyi Eso, the one with punctured bags.

The one who opened the quiver and swallowed two hundred arrows through the gullet, and with ease he vomited the two hundred arrows. You inhabited the house, lived in the wild, occupied the deep forest, and found abode on trees and in the passages. Why is this so? Because the tribe of the Eso made their bones from hunting in the evil forest.

Eso Ikoyi, like it or not, you have no say in this matter for it's time for battle. Ikoyi showed up at the battle scene and he saw diplomats oiling the peace deal. For this reason, he drove a sword into his entrails.

Your forebears died in a mangled shape. Your father slept in a disheveled heap. Your fathers dangled on a tree to deceive.

Unceasing fighters, sleeping sideways,

Snapping back to life at a moment's notice.

The son of those who died for birds to feast upon.

Hear it again: when they died in the citadel of ancient Oyo,

The King would be informed of their demise,

And the king would give instructions for their open-yard interment.

When their fathers died in the citadel of ancient Oyo,

The king would order their burial at the tip of the room.

When it got to the turn of Eso Ikoyi,

The son of the basket that basks under the gaze of rebellion,

He also died in the citadel of ancient Oyo.

The king gave instructions for an open-yard interment, but Eso said his soul shall not sleep there.

The king ordered his burial at the tip of the room,

But Ikoyi said his soul shall not slip there.

For this reason, they consulted the oracle.

The oracle told them to summon the smith of Offa,

The oracle told them to bring the owner of the anvil of Ijagbo,

They are to forge a brass coffin and place it in the placc of abundant mushrooms.

Therefore, when the household fools and village wags say that Eso had no place to sleep,

This shall be our retort.

Unceasing fighters, sons of those who died for birds to feast upon,

In death, they lay in the place of abundant mushrooms.

Their brass coffins gleaming, a symbol of their defiance,

A testament to their spirit, unbroken and timeless.

Curtain closes

EXEUNT

www.ingramcontent.com/pod-product-compliance
Lightning Source LLC
La Vergne TN
LVHW010455160826
845677LV00012B/2496

9789785207743